Silver from the Sea

Also by Ruth Tooze

AMERICA

Silver from the Sea

BY RUTH TOOZE

Illustrated by Kurt Wiese

NEW YORK • THE VIKING PRESS

PRINTED IN THE U. S. A. BY KELLOGG & BULKELEY

To

SANDY, TOM, MARGARET, NANCY, AND JEAN
Who Also Found Silver in the Sea

Ti Nang Dinh raced up and down the beach this bright sunny morning. He was barefoot, as all the children were on the Long Hai beach of the China Sea in Vietnam, where it is always warm. He had a long, floppy piece of seaweed tied to his back, and it made a wonderful tail. He really was a dragon come up out of the far pools to talk to the silver sea in front of him. The sun danced on every wave and made them shine silver instead of blue. Surely

7

this was a good omen, for this day was his day to collect the silver from the sea when the long haul brought in the fish.

He flipped his tail and ran to the edge of the water and stopped.

"Oh, Silver Waters, this is my day to be first boy to collect the fish. Oh, Silver Waters, will you send in much silver, many fish? I know some days you have not much silver to send, but today, oh, today, please send in nets bulging with silver, many fish jumping and dancing. Today is my Fish Day."

He turned and flipped his tail once more. He opened his mouth, shooting his tongue in and out like the real dragon of the pools, and ran in and out of the water.

He ran.

He danced.

He laughed.

He shouted to the silver waters.

"Oh, Silver Waters, I'm really just Ti Nang Dinh. I just pretend to be the Dragon and do

magic. So, Silver Waters, give to Ti Nang Dinh much silver on my first day to be center boy when the fish come in."

"Dinh! Dinh!"

He could hear his mother calling. There she was with the group of women sitting quietly on the beach. Surely it was not yet time to start the long haul. So he ran farther away along the edge of the water.

"Dinh! Dinh! Don't you hear me?"

Yes, he heard. Maybe she wanted to tell him when they would begin to pull. So he ran to the group of women.

"Dinh, I have left my rope at home. You must run home and get it for me. Quickly, Dinh, run."

His jaw dropped. He wouldn't let the tears show, so he swallowed hard.

"Oh, Dinh," said his aunt. "Don't be so important. We know you are first boy at the fish today, but we won't start for an hour, and the pull takes two hours or more. You know that, Dinh. There is plenty of time for you to run home to get mother's tying rope."

She was probably right, but he couldn't stand to be away from the silver waters one minute this day. He knew he had no choice but to go. He looked up at his mother, but he could not smile. He said, "I'll run all the way and be back soon."

She smiled and nodded. "You'll make it."

Dinh took off his seaweed tail and ran across the sand, past his uncles rolling up the long nets on

the wooden horses, and through the low bushes to the road. He ran and ran all the way home. There lay the rope on the little porch in front of his small wooden house. He grabbed it up quickly, but he was so out of breath he could not start back. When he sat down to rest for a minute, his sister saw him and came out to join him.

13

"Why are you here, Dinh? Did you forget this is your fish day?"

Forget? What did she think he lived for?

"No, silly, I did not forget. Our mother forgot. She forgot her tying rope and sent me back to get it. I ran so hard, I am out of breath. Now I am all right and I'm going to run back with the rope."

"Don't run, Dinh, don't wear yourself out. You need all your strength to be center boy when the fish come in. Walk back. There is plenty of time."

Dinh walked as long as he knew she could see him, but then he broke into a run, fearing the long pull might start early today. It just might today. Soon he was beyond the little village. He scrambled through the low bushes, ran past his uncles, who were still putting up the heavy black nets, and reached the group of women, who were still sitting quietly on the sand talking and idly letting the sand run through their fingers.

"You see," said his aunt. But his mother put up her hand and took the rope as she smiled. "Thank you, my Dinh. Rest here a little. It was a long run."

Dinh sank down on his knees beside her, but he couldn't stay long. He ran back to his uncles, who were piling the nets.

"May I help?" he asked.

"Not yet, Dinh," said one of his uncles. "You will be first boy at the fish today. It takes a small one to get into the center net. But to pile the nets takes a big strong man. Some day you will have to roll out the nets to dry on the sand, then pile them

16

on the wooden horses, as we are doing now, and
load them onto the boats to be taken far out and
let down into the sea. That is the work of every
strong man, every day in our village. When you
grow up, it will be your work too." His uncle talked
on as he moved the wooden horse along and piled
more net on it.

"Dinh."

"Yes, Uncle."

"Remember, today, not to hurry too much. Watch the circle of the nets get smaller and smaller and nearer the shore. Then take your two pails and walk straight to the center, where the fish will be thickest, and fill your pails. Tong and Fan will be waiting with their baskets. Empty your pails quickly and go right back to the center where the fish are thickest—over and over and over. Pay no attention to all the pushing, shouting men and other children. You are center boy today. They know. Hold your place. May it be a day of many fish!"

"Yes, Uncle."

Dinh turned away, and walked slowly across the

sand. He saw the women still sitting idly on the
sand. There lay his seaweed tail. He kicked it aside.
Playing dragon held no more magic for him, even
though the sun shone brighter and every wave tip
sparkled. He stretched out his arms.

"Silver Waters, Silver Waters, remember this is
my Fish Day. Bring me silver, bring me fishes,
lots of fishes."

He ran into the water, turned a somersault, and ran out. He ran in again, dived into a wave, and let it carry him back to the shore. This was the kind of play he did every day, but today ought to be different, his Fish Day. But it was just like every other day of waiting, running, playing. The other boys were coming to the beach now, waving seaweed, dancing in and out of the water. Nuong slapped his shoulder to make him come and play tag. Not today, he couldn't. Not today, his Fish Day.

20

He watched the water.
He watched the women.
He watched the water.
He watched the women.
Would the long pull never begin?

He did not see the signal, but suddenly all the women were standing. They picked up the big rope that had been lying on the sand coming in from the water. His mother walked down to the water's edge and tied herself to the big rope with her tying rope which he had brought to her, dug her heels into the wet sand, and leaned her body back as she held the rope. His aunt tied herself to the rope about three yards back of his mother, dug

her heels in, and leaned back. All the other women spaced themselves, tied themselves to the rope, dug their heels in, and leaned back. Slowly, slowly they began to pull, all their bodies bent back from the pull of the water. The long pull was on. As enough rope to make a coil came up at the end, the end woman untied herself and ran forward to tie herself onto the rope ahead of his mother.

Pull! Pull! Pull!

The next woman let more rope down on the coil, untied herself, and ran ahead to tie herself onto the rope.

Pull! Pull! Pull!

The next woman let more rope down on the coil and ran ahead to tie herself on the rope.

Pull! Pull! Pull!

On and on they went, bending themselves against the pull of the water, letting more rope down on the coil, untying themselves, running ahead to tie themselves on again and strain their bodies taut with the rope. The long pull to bring in the fish fell into a rhythm and went right on.

No one spoke.

More children and other women came and watched.

The women on the rope never stopped or changed their rhythm.

Pull! Pull! Pull! Let down rope, untie yourself, run ahead, and tie yourself on again.

Pull! Pull! Pull! Let down rope, untie yourself, run ahead, and tie yourself on again.

The second great coil was started, the third, the fourth.

One hour passed.

Another hour passed.

Pull! Pull! Pull!

Sometimes Dinh stood beside his mother, moved slowly back with her as the rope came in, and ran ahead with her as she tied herself on at the water's edge.

Then he saw the others. That group of women at the other end of the big nets had been so far up the beach, no one had noticed them. It was always like that. The first group were the important group. They began the long pull. The second smaller group didn't begin their pulling until the first group had been pulling an hour or more. Now they pulled their rope the same way. Slowly they moved along the shore, nearer, nearer to the first group. This is the way they pulled the ropes to bring in the huge nets.

Holding his two pails, Dinh stood between the ropes right at the water's edge, watching, watching. His heart pounded.

His Fish Day!

His uncles finished piling the dry nets on the wooden horses and came down to the beach. All the men came down to the beach now. Soon everyone from the village was on the beach.

Suddenly his strongest uncle ran ahead of the lead woman of the first group and tied himself to the rope. Other men replaced some of the women.

They pulled with all their strength. The rope piled
up faster and faster.

There were the nets, the big black nets!

Were they full of fish, silver fish?

Dinh never moved as he watched that black half circle bob in and out of the blue water. The men and women pulled hard and fast.

The women at the other end pulled hard and fast.

Pull! Pull! Pull!

Faster! Faster! Faster!

The big half circle of the nets moved nearer and nearer.

Now Dinh lifted his two pails and walked into the shallow water, standing halfway between the ropes. Other boys crowded around him. He remembered what his uncle had said and paid no attention to them.

The men of the village ran into the water shouting, "It's heavy! A big haul today, lots of fish. A big haul!"

Dinh could hardly see what was coming, through those blurred eyes of his. Why couldn't he keep back those tears? But he faced the sea and no one saw them.

"Silver Waters! Silver Waters!" he cried, but no one heard him.

Now the strong men took the ropes and pulled mightily. Dinh watched the half circle of the nets grow smaller and smaller as it came nearer the shore. He walked farther into the water, holding his two pails.

The first end of the net was in! A few little silver fish jumped and danced in it.

Then the big center sections came. The men could scarcely pull them in. They were so full that no fish, big or little, could jump or dance. Dinh was right there in front of the very center. One man pushed some of the load into Dinh's two pails.

Silver fish! Silver fish!

Dinh turned around and emptied his pails into
Tong's and Fan's baskets and ran back with his
pails. They were full in a second. He emptied them
and ran back. They were full in a second. Over
and over and over. Other children filled their pails
too, but Dinh was center boy and had center place
to get the best of the haul. His arms ached so that
he thought he couldn't hold the pails, but he did.
The men helped him.

All around him, men and children were in the water, many getting fish, many just screaming in excitement, the strong ones holding the nets so they could be emptied.

Everyone worked at the last as the big haul came in. They shouted and screamed and laughed as they held the strong black nets and emptied them of their heavy load of fish—big fish, little fish, even starfish and jellyfish, just to throw away.

But there were plenty of silver fish for the market today.

At last there were only a few little ones jumping around.

Dinh walked out of the water with his last pails half full. He didn't bother to empty them into the baskets, but walked straight over to his grandmother. There she stood with a circle of baskets around her, setting up her market. Dinh gave her the half-full pails.

36

She quickly sorted them and tossed each kind into its own basket. "You had a big Fish Day on your Fish Day, Dinh. Today's market is a good market."

Dinh looked up and said, "My Fish Day. Good. Much silver, many fish. Good!"

She nodded.

The customers crowded around her. She held
her scales and sold fish, little fish, big fish, many
fish, silver fish.

38

He couldn't see his mother or the women. They
had gone home, their day's work over.

His uncles were spreading the heavy black nets
out to dry in long rows on the sand, their day's
work begun.

His grandmother was selling fish, and more fish.

Dinh ached all over but he wouldn't sit down.
He walked to the edge of the sea.

The long pull was over.

The big haul was in.

He stretched out his arms.

"Silver Waters, Silver Waters, thank you for many fish, for silver fish today, my Fish Day."